To Flynn,
   I love you so much
e we'll really enjoy this
book together.
      All love mummy
                    XX
                    XX

ÆSOP'S FABLES

Illustrated by
Patricia Ludlow

Brown Watson
ENGLAND

CONTENTS

First published 1999 by Brown Watson,
76 Fleckney Road, Kibworth Beauchamp,
Leicestershire LE8 0HG
© 1999 Brown Watson
ISBN: 0-7097-1312-6

THE CROW AND THE PITCHER

Almost dying with thirst, a crow found a pitcher with a little water in the bottom of it. The crow wasn't strong enough to tip the pitcher over, or to break it so that she could get at the water. Then, seeing some small pebbles nearby, she dropped them one by one into the pitcher. Slowly, this made the water level rise higher and higher inside the pitcher, until it was so high that the crow could reach it with her beak and easily drink to quench her thirst.

MORAL
Necessity is the mother of invention.

THE BOYS AND THE FROGS

The frogs had a happy and peaceful life in a pond until one day some boys began to amuse themselves by throwing stones into the water. The boys enjoyed what they thought was good fun, but the frogs didn't like it. There were so many stones flying through the air and splashing into the water, the frogs feared for their lives. Some hid behind rocks, while others dived to the bottom of the pond. Finally, one brave frog popped his head out of the water and called out to the boys:

"Oh, please stop! Your game may be fun to you, but it's putting our lives in danger!"

MORAL
What we do in fun can sometimes be of harm to others.

THE DOG AND THE MEAT

A dog ran off with a piece of meat stolen from the butcher's shop. Crossing over a river on his way home, he looked down at his own reflection in the water. He thought the reflection was another dog with another piece of meat and decided he may as well have both pieces. But, as he opened his mouth to snap at the reflection, he dropped his piece of meat into the water. It was carried away by the river and so he lost all of his meat.

MORAL
Try to grasp the shadow and you will lose the real thing.

HERCULES AND THE WAGONNER

The rain was pouring down and the wheels of the farmer's wagon became stuck in the very thick mud.

His horses came to a standstill, unable to move forward. The farmer jumped down from his wagon, but made no attempt himself to help move the wagon wheels. Instead, he bent upon his knees and prayed to the Heavens that the great god Hercules would come and help him.

Hercules did appear, but only to advise the farmer to try first helping himself. So, the farmer bent down and put his own shoulder to one of the wagon's wheels. He pushed and he shoved and urged on his horses. Gradually, the wheels turned and the wagon moved forward. Soon they were clear and the farmer was once more riding on his wagon, having learned a very good lesson.

MORAL
Heaven helps those who first help themselves.

6

THE WOMAN AND THE FAT HEN

An old woman kept a hen which, without fail, laid one egg every morning. The eggs were of the highest quality and the old woman was able to sell them for a very good price.

"If only my hen would lay two eggs a day," she thought, "my income would be doubled!"

So, she began feeding her hen twice as much corn each day.

Unfortunately all this extra food made the hen grow so fat and contented that it became lazy and gave up laying eggs altogether!

MORAL
However carefully the future is worked out, things may not go as planned.

THE COCKEREL AND THE JEWEL

Searching for scraps of food, a cockerel was scratching up the earth in the farmyard. Suddenly, he came upon a precious jewel, shining and glittering with many colours. Not knowing its real value, he did not know what to do with it.

"You are certainly a very fine object for those who might appreciate your true value," sighed the cockerel, "but I'd prefer a single grain of corn."

MORAL
The beautiful value of an object is in the eye of the beholder.

THE HARE AND THE TORTOISE

The hare was making fun of the tortoise's short legs and the way he moved so slowly. "I'll beat you in a race any day," smiled the tortoise to the hare, who accepted the challenge to race.

It was decided that the fox should choose the course and decide the winner. The race began and the hare sped off. The tortoise moved off very, very slowly.

Soon, the hare was so far ahead and sure of winning, that he stopped to rest and fell asleep.

Later, while he still slept, the tortoise passed by and went on slowly to cross the finishing line. All the animals cheered as the fox proclaimed him the winner.

When the hare woke up and saw no sign of the tortoise, he ran as fast as he could to the finishing line. But, by then, the tortoise was the winner!

MORAL
Being slow but sure can sometimes defeat those who are swift.

THE WOLF SMELLS DINNER

A wolf was attracted to the shepherd's cottage by the smell of freshly cooked food. He peeped around the door and saw the shepherd's wife serving her family with a joint of roast lamb for dinner. "It smells delicious," growled the wolf, "but what an outcry there'd be if ever they caught me eating such a meal!"

MORAL
Some criticise others for the things they do themselves.

THE TRAVELLERS AND THE BEAR

Two friends were travelling on foot along a forest path when a huge bear leapt out from the bushes in front of them. Thinking only of himself, one traveller climbed up a tall tree to safety.

Left alone, the other traveller knew he was no match for the mighty bear.

So, remembering some say that a bear will not touch a dead body, he lay quite still upon the ground and pretended to be dead.

The bear sniffed all around the man's head. Then, satisfied he seemed to be dead, the bear walked away. The man in the tree climbed down. He had seen everything and said, "That bear seemed to whisper something in your ear. What did it say?"

His friend replied, "Oh, nothing really – it simply advised me to avoid the company of those who desert their friends in time of need."

MORAL
Misfortune can put true friendship to the test.

THE SHEPHERD BOY AND THE WOLF

Looking after his flock of sheep, a shepherd boy often used to amuse himself by crying out: "Wolf! Wolf!" The boy laughed at the sight of villagers who, thinking his sheep were being attacked, ran to his rescue.

The boy thought this very funny, until one day a wolf really did come to attack his sheep. He cried out, but no one came to help him. The villagers thought it was just another trick. They paid no attention to his cries and the sheep were left at the mercy of a real wolf.

MORAL
Those who tell lies are not believed, even when they speak the truth.

THE MONKEY AND THE DOLPHIN

In ancient times, Greek seafarers often took their pet monkeys and dogs with them to provide company and amusement during long voyages.

One man and his pet monkey became separated when their ship sank during a great storm, just off the port of Athens. It just so happened that at that time, the dolphins of the sea were very friendly with all the seafarers from Athens. So, they swam to the rescue of the drowning sailors and carried them on their backs to safety.

One dolphin mistook the drowning monkey for a human being. She took him on her back and headed towards the shore. They were getting near to Pireaus, which was the name of the port of Athens, when the dolphin asked the monkey if he lived in Athens. The monkey told her he belonged to one of the most important families in Athens.

"In that case, you must know Pireaus very well?" asked the dolphin.

"Surely I do," the monkey told her. "He's one of my very best friends."

Realising the monkey was trying to fool her, the angry dolphin dived deep into the water and left the monkey to his fate.

MORAL
One lie will lead to another and eventually seal your doom.

13

THE MILKMAID AND HER PAIL

The milkmaid balanced a pail of milk upon her head as she walked home from the cowshed. She was dreaming of what she would do with the money she would earn from the milk. "From the milk I will make butter," she thought. "From the money I get from selling the butter, I will buy a lot of eggs for hatching and my yard will become full of young chicks. Then, when I sell the chicks, I'll buy me a new dress to wear to the fair."

The milkmaid began to think how pretty

THE HEN AND THE CAT

A sly old cat dressed up as a nurse and visited the sick hen as she sat upon her nest. "How are you today?" purred the cat, as bit by bit she moved closer to the nest. "Are you in need of anything?" she asked the hen. "I hope you're feeling better."

"Thank you," replied the hen. "If you'll be good enough to leave me alone, I'm sure I'll soon be well again."

MORAL
Uninvited guests are often most welcome when they leave.

she would look at the fair. She imagined how all the young men would come courting her, only to be sent on their way by a toss of her proud head.

In fact, she was so lost in her daydreaming that she really did toss her head. The pail of milk wobbled and fell from her head. The milk soaked into the ground and soon disappeared, as did all her dreams of eggs and chicks, butter and money, her new dress and all her pride.

MORAL
Don't count your chickens before they've hatched.

15

THE MOUSE, THE CAT AND THE ROOSTER

The young mouse returned from his first journey into the outside world with a tale of two creatures he'd met. One he described as a fearsome monster wearing a bright red crown. It flapped its arms about and scratched up the earth with its big claws. It threw back its head to give out terrifying screeches from its big yellow jaws.

"Oh, that was only old Rooster the Cockerel," his mother told the young mouse.

"Well, he frightened me so much," said the young mouse, "that I fled in fright just as I was about to speak to that other creature who had a furry coat and a pretty face with such a friendly smile."

"Gracious!" cried Mother Mouse, "That was the cat, our greatest enemy who catches mice and eats them up. Keep well away from the cat!"

MORAL
Do not judge a person only by their outward appearance.

THE WAITING GAME

Some shepherds had hidden their packed lunches inside a hollow tree. Later, a hungry fox came by and smelt the food.

His stomach was so empty that he was thin enough to squeeze into the tree through a hole in the trunk. He ate all the packed lunches, but his stomach was so full that he was not able to squeeze back through the hole and out of the tree trunk.

"Please help me!" he cried out to another passing fox. The fox could only advise him to stay where he was, without food, until he became as thin as when he had squeezed in.

MORAL
Sometimes only the passing of time itself can heal life's problems.

THE STAG'S REFLECTION

When the stag bent to drink from a pool, he saw his reflection in the crystal clear water. Looking at the watery picture of himself, he admired the mighty antlers set upon his noble head.

"It's a pity about my long knobbly legs," he sighed. At that moment, a hungry panther, who'd been watching from behind a bush, made a powerful spring towards him. In a flash, the stag turned and took off at speed to flee from the panther. The stag's powerful legs soon took him safely ahead of the panther. Then, quite suddenly, the stag saw that he was being chased into the forest. There, the antlers of which he'd been so proud, became entangled in the branches of the trees. Only then did he realise that the strong legs, which he had so disliked, had carried him to safety only for him to be caught because of the antlers of which he'd been so proud.

MORAL
We often admire decorative things but dislike the things which are useful.

18

THE HAWK AND THE PIGEONS

The hawk was always swooping around the shed in which the pigeons lived. If he could catch only a single pigeon, it would make him a very good meal.

Because his attacks failed, the hawk decided upon a cunning plan.

"Why do you live your lives worrying that I might attack you?" he called out to the pigeons. "Make me your King and I won't bother you any more. I can live in your shed and frighten off all your other attackers such as the kites and the falcons."

The pigeons decided to trust the hawk and agreed that he should become their King and protector.

Then, as soon as he was allowed to live in their shed, he began his reign by eating one pigeon each day.

"It serves us right," said one pigeon, even though it was his turn to be eaten!

MORAL
Sometimes the remedy is worse than the illness itself.

THE FOX AND THE GOAT

A fox had fallen into the well and couldn't get out. A thirsty goat came along and, upon hearing the fox call for help, looked down into the well and asked the fox if the water was good. "The water is so good that I cannot get enough of it," replied the fox and invited the goat to join him.

The goat promptly jumped down into the well and drank his fill. Only then did the fox tell him that now they were both trapped, with no way of escape. The cunning fox explained that they could escape if the goat stood up on his back legs, with his front feet against the wall. Then, the fox would be able to run up the goat's back and reach the top of the well. "Then, I'll go and fetch some help and get you out of the well, also," added the fox.

The goat did as he suggested and the fox ran up his back. But, when the fox jumped out of the well, he began to run away. He called out that he was in a hurry for an important meeting. "Hey, what about me?" the goat cried after him. "We had an agreement!" The fox did come back, but only to tell the goat: "If you had half as many brains as the hairs in your beard, you'd never have jumped down the well in the first place. You should have made sure there was a way to get back up again. I must dash away now or I'll be late for my meeting. Bye! Bye!"

With that, the fox was gone, leaving the goat down the well.

MORAL
Always look before you leap.

THE TRUMPETER TAKEN PRISONER

A young trumpeter who had blown the bugle calls sending his regiment into battle, was captured by the enemy army. "Spare me!" pleaded the trumpeter, as he begged for mercy from his captors. "I haven't killed anyone, for I do not carry weapons of any sort. All I have is my bugle."

"But that is a good reason why we should not spare you," replied his captors. "Even though you don't fight yourself, your bugle calls send orders to your soldiers to rise up, to fight and to shed blood!"

MORAL
Those who encourage others to fight are no better than those who take part in the fighting.

THE MOUSE AND THE LION

Scampering her way through the forest, a tiny mouse ran over the nose of a sleeping lion by accident. This woke the lion from his slumbers. He was very cross and angrily scooped up the mouse in his mighty paw.

"Oh, mighty lion, King of Beasts, please spare my life!" pleaded the mouse. "I didn't mean to wake you up. It was an accident. Let me go and one day I will repay your kindness." The lion could not imagine how a mouse could ever be of help to him. But, he was in a generous mood and let the mouse go free. Days later, the mouse heard the lion's mighty roar echo through the forest. She ran to find the lion trapped in the ropes of a hunter's net. He was unable to escape. "Don't worry, I'll soon have you free," squeaked the little mouse.

The mouse chewed and chewed on one of the main ropes of the net until it parted and the lion was able to struggle free.

"I don't think you believed me when I said I would repay your kindness," the mouse told the grateful lion.

MORAL
Even the weakest can repay kindness by the greatest.

SOUR GRAPES

The hungry fox tried again and again to reach the bunch of grapes hanging from a vine, high up on a fence. They were too high up for him to reach. So, he walked away, telling himself: "Ugh! They were not ripe enough to eat, anyway!"

MORAL
Those who fail to get what they want often become critical of that which they cannot possess.

VENUS AND THE CAT

When a cat fell in love with a handsome young man, she prayed to the god Venus to change her into a girl so that she could win his total affection. Because Venus felt sorry for the cat, she answered her prayers and the young man instantly fell in love with the beautiful girl who appeared before him.

They were soon married and lived happily together in the young man's home. Venus was delighted that things had worked out so well, but still wanted to be sure and positive that she had changed the cat completely into a girl. So, Venus placed a tiny mouse in front of the girl. Instantly, like the cat she really was, the girl pounced upon the mouse as though to eat the creature.

THE WOLF AND THE HERON

The greedy wolf swallowed his food so quickly that a bone became stuck deep in his throat. The wolf howled with pain, but no creature dare come near to help him. Only when he offered a rich reward did a heron take pity on him. The heron popped her head into the wolf's mouth and reached down his throat with her beak. She got hold of the bone and gently removed it, relieving the wolf of his terrible pain. Then, the heron politely asked the wolf for the reward he had promised. "Reward!" exclaimed the wolf. "Your life is your reward, for not many place their heads into the mouth of a wolf and live to tell the tale!"

MORAL
Expect no reward if you help the wicked.

"Oh, that sort of
behaviour will never do
for a human being!"
exclaimed Venus, as she
turned the girl back
into a cat again.

MORAL
*However hard you try,
you cannot change one's
basic nature.*

MERCURY AND THE WOODSMAN

A woodsman was chopping down a tree on the riverbank when he let his axe slip and it vanished into the water. The woodsman was very upset. It was the only axe he had and he needed it to earn his living. He was too poor to buy another. He dropped to his knees and held his head in despair. Suddenly, the god Mercury rose up from the water in front of him. After hearing the woodsman's story, Mercury plunged into the water and came up holding a golden axe.

"Is this your axe?" he asked the woodsman, who told him no, it was not.

Mercury placed the golden axe on the riverbank and came up for the second time holding an axe made of silver.

"No, that's not mine either," said the honest woodsman. "Mine is just an ordinary axe with a wooden handle."

Mercury dived for the third time and the woodsman was overjoyed to see him come up holding the very axe he'd lost.

"I admire your honesty," Mercury told the woodsman, "and as a special reward you may keep both the gold and silver axes as well as your own."

News of the woodsman's good fortune spread around nearby villages and soon other men decided to go in search of riches from the god Mercury. Each hid his own axe in nearby bushes and in turn knelt to pray for help from Mercury. Mercury listened to their tales of woe and to each he showed a golden axe which they immediately claimed to be their own. Mercury didn't give them a golden axe, but they had a good telling off about their dishonest ways and sent back to their homes. What's more, when they returned next day to collect their own axes, they were nowhere to be found.

MORAL
Honesty is the best policy.

THE FOX AND THE LION

The first time a fox ever set eyes upon a lion, he was so terrified that he almost died of fright. The second time he met a lion, the fox was still afraid, but just about able to hide his fear. By this time, the fox was beginning to think that maybe the lion wasn't so frightening after all. So, when he met the lion for the third time, the fox walked straight up to him and began asking the King of Beasts some very personal questions.

MORAL
Familiarity breeds contempt.

THE GOATHERD AND THE GOATS

Snow was falling, so the goatherd drove his goats into a cave for shelter. He found a herd of wild goats already inside. Because they appeared stronger than his own herd, he fed them, and neglected his own goats.

When the weather was clear enough for them to leave, his own goats had died of hunger and the wild goats ran off before he could catch them.

MORAL
Neglect old friends for new and you may end up losing both.

THE FARMER AND THE STORK

Cranes had been eating a farmer's newly sown corn, so he set up a net to catch them. Next day, he found a stork among the cranes caught in the net. "Please spare me!" cried the stork. "I'm not a crane, but a poor innocent stork. I haven't eaten any of your corn. I'm a good bird and look after my family..." "Bah!" interrupted the farmer, "I only know that I caught you in the company of the birds who stole my corn, so you must share their fate!"

MORAL
Birds of a feather are judged to flock together.

THE OX AND THE FROGS

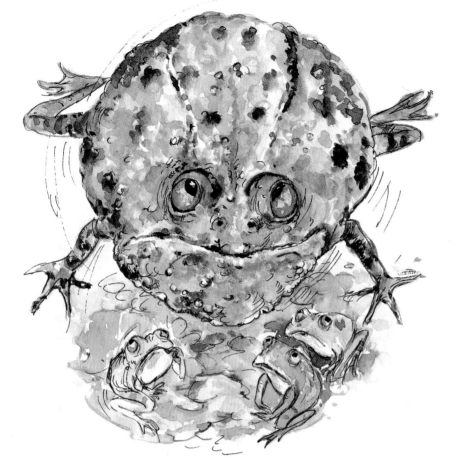

When the ox splashed into the pool for a drink, his feet almost crushed a family of young frogs at play. They rushed to tell Mother Frog of their narrow escape from what they thought had been a great monster.

"How big was the monster?" asked Mother Frog, puffing herself up as much as she could.

"Oh, much bigger than that!" said her children.

"Well, how about this?" cried Mother Frog, puffing herself out even bigger again.

"We're afraid you would burst before you were even half the monster's size," cried the young frogs.

Sadly, this is just what Mother Frog did. She huffed and puffed with one more effort until – bang! She exploded into the air and was gone for ever.

MORAL
Everyone has a limit to the greatness they can achieve.

THE OLD WOMAN AND HER MAIDS

Two young house-maids lived with a mean old woman who wanted all the work she could get out of them for the low wages she paid.

Every morning at sunrise, the crowing of the cockerel woke the woman and she woke the maids to begin their long, hard working day. The maids decided the cockerel was the real problem, because he woke the woman every morning in the first place. So, they gave the cockerel to a farmer and looked forward to some good nights of well earned rest. But, without the cockerel to wake her, the old woman was afraid she might oversleep. She became mixed up, mistaking the hours of day and night. She woke her maids at all hours, even as early as midnight, to begin another long day's work.

MORAL
Plots which are too cunning can sometimes defeat their purpose.

THE BLIND MAN AND THE WOLF CUB

Once there was a blind man who only had to touch an animal to know what sort of creature it was.

To test his powers, some friends placed a young wolf cub on his lap. The blind man examined the cub carefully with his hands. He wasn't sure about the animal. He was uncertain whether it was a wolf or fox cub or the puppy of a dog.

"I am certain of one thing though," he told the little creature. "When you grow up I don't think I'd trust you with a flock of sheep."

MORAL
Evil natures can be recognised by physical qualities.